Oliver Goldsmith, James Hook

The Hermit

Oliver Goldsmith, James Hook

The Hermit

ISBN/EAN: 9783337395087

Printed in Europe, USA, Canada, Australia, Japan

Cover: Foto ©Andreas Hilbeck / pixelio.de

More available books at **www.hansebooks.com**

THE HERMIT

Written by the late Celebrated D.ʳ Goldsmith,

Set to Music by

James & Hook.

—— Adapted for ——

Two VIOLINS, VOICE & HARPSICHORD.

Opera XXIV ——————————————— Price 4.ˢ

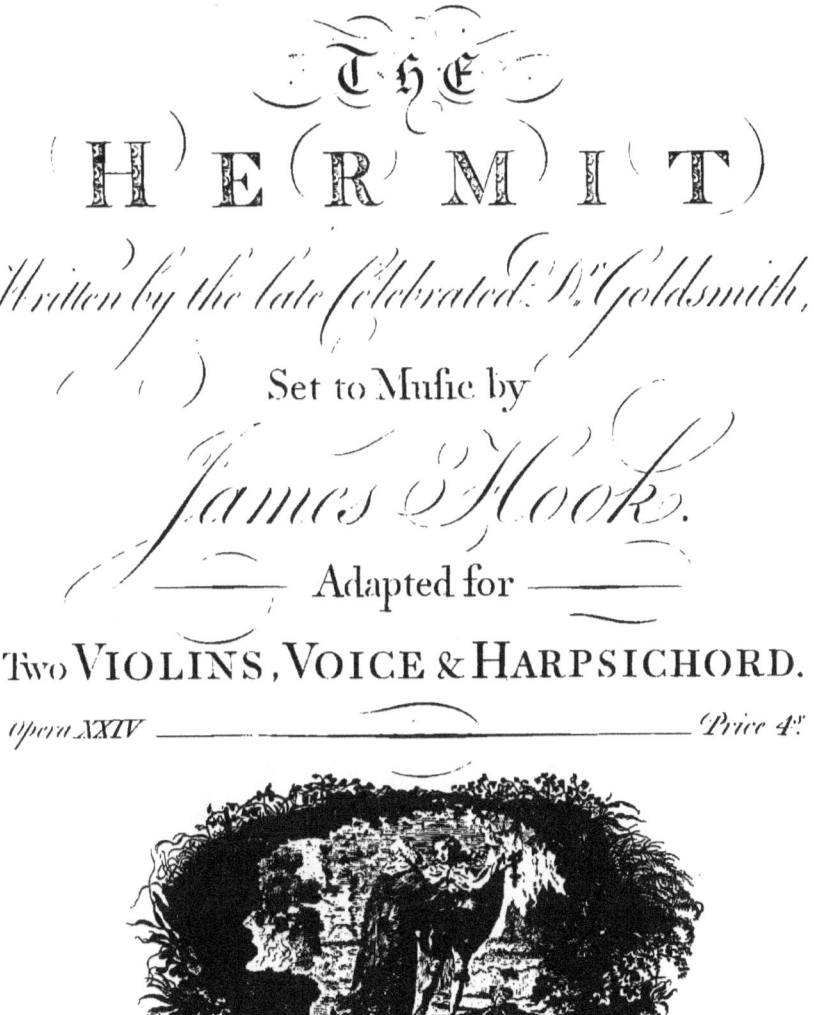

LONDON

Printed for S. A. & P. Thompson. N.º 75 S.ᵗ Pauls Church Yard.

THE HERMIT.
By D.ʳ Goldſmith.

"Turn, gentle Hermit, of the Dale,
"And guide my lonely Way
"To where yon'ſaper chears the Vale,
"With hoſpitable Ray.

"For here, forlorn and loſt, I tread,
"With fainting Steps, and ſlow;
"Where Wilds, immeaſurably ſpread,
"Seem length'ning as I go.

"Forbear, my Son,"(the Hermit cries,)
"To tempt the dang'rous Gloom,
"For yonder faithleſs Phantom flies
"To lure thee to thy Doom.

"Here to the houſeleſs Child of Want
"My Door is open ſtill;
"And tho' my Portion is but ſcant,
"I give it with good Will.

"Then turn to Night, and freely ſhare
"Whate'er my Cell beſtows;
"My ruſhy Couch, and frugal Fare,
"My Bleſſing, and Repoſe.

"No Flocks that range the Valley free
"To Slaughter I condemn;
"Taught by that Pow'r that pities me,
"I learn to pity them.

"But from the Mountain's graſſy Side
"A guiltleſs Feaſt I bring;
"A Scrip with Herbs and Fruit ſupply'd,
"And Water from the Spring.

"Then, Pilgrim, turn, thy Cares forego;
"All earth-born Cares are wrong:
"Man wants but little here below,
"Nor wants that little long."

Soft as the Dew from Heav'n deſcends
His gentle Accents fell;
The modeſt Stranger lowly bends,
And follows to the Cell.

Far in a Wilderneſs obſcure
The lonely Manſion lay;
A Refuge to the neighb'ring Poor,
And Strangers led aſtray.

No Stores beneath its humble Thatch
Requir'd a Maſter's Care;
The Wicket, op'ning with a Latch,
Receiv'd the harmleſs Pair.

And now, when buſy Crowds retire
To take their ev'ning Reſt,
The Hermit trimm'd his little Fire,
And chear'd his penſive Gueſt;

And ſpread his vegetable Store,
And gaily preſt and ſmil'd;
And, ſkill'd in legendary Lore,
The ling'ring Hours beguil'd.

Around in ſympathetic Mirth
Its Tricks the Kitten tries;
The Cricket chirrups in the Hearth,
The crackling Faggot flies.

But nothing could a Charm impart,
To ſooth the Stranger's Woe;
For Grief was heavy at his Heart,
And Tears began to flow.

His riſing Cares the Hermit ſpy'd,
With anſw'ring Care oppreſt:
"And whence, unhappy Youth," (he cry'd,)
"The Sorrows of thy Breaſt?

"From better Habitations ſpurn'd,
"Reluctant doſt thou rove;
"Or grieve for Friendſhip unreturn'd,
"Or unregarded Love?

"Alas! the Joys that Fortune brings
"Are trifling, and decay;
"And thoſe, who prize the paltry Things,
"More trifling ſtill than they.

"And what is Friendſhip, but a Name,
"A Charm that lulls to ſleep;
"A Shade that follows Wealth, or Fame,
"And leaves the Wretch to weep?

"And Love is ſtill an emptier Sound,
"The modern fair one's Jeſt:
"On Earth unſeen, or only found
"To warm the Turtle's Neſt.

"For Shame, fond Youth, thy Sorrows huſh,
"And ſpurn the Sex," he ſaid:
But while he ſpoke, a riſing Bluſh
His love-lorn Gueſt betray'd.

Surpriz'd, he ſees new Beauties riſe,
Swift mantling to the View;
Like Colours o'er the morning Skies,
As bright, as tranſient too.

The baſhful Look, the riſing Breaſt,
Alternate ſpread Alarms;
The lovely Stranger ſtands confeſt
A Maid in all her Charms.

"And ah! forgive a Stranger rude,
"A Wretch forlorn" (ſhe cry'd,)
"Whoſe Feet unhallow'd thus intrude
"Where Heav'n and you reſide.

"But let a Maid thy Pity ſhare,
"Whom Love has taught to ſtray;
"Who ſeeks for reſt, but finds Deſpair
"Companion of her Way.

"My Father liv'd beſide the Tyne,
"A wealthy Lord was he;
"And all his Wealth was mark'd as mine,
"He had but only me.

"To win me from his tender Arms,
"Unnumber'd Suitors came;
"Who praiſ'd me for imputed Charms,
"And felt, or feign'd a Flame.

"Each Hour a mercenary Crowd
"With richeſt Proffers ſtrove;
"Among the reſt young Edwin bow'd,
"But never talk'd of Love.

"In humble, ſimpleſt Habit clad,
"No Wealth or Pow'r had he;
"Wiſdom and Worth were all he had;
"But theſe were all to me.

"The Bloſſom op'ning to the Day,
"The Dews of Heav'n refin'd,
"Could Nought of Purity diſplay,
"To emulate his Mind.

"The Dew, the Bloſſoms of the Tree,
"With Charms inconſtant ſhine;
"Their Charms were his, but woe to me.
"Their Conſtancy was mine.

"For ſtill I try'd each fickle Art,
"Importunate and vain;
"And while his Paſſion touch'd my Heart,
"I triumph'd in his Pain

"Till quite dejected with my Scorn,
"He left me to my Pride,
"And ſought a Solitude forlorn,
In ſecret, where he dy'd.

"But mine the Sorrow, mine the Fault,
"And well my Life ſhall pay;
"I'll ſeek the Solitude he ſought,
"And ſtretch me where he lay.

"And there forlorn, deſpairing hid,
"I'll lay me down, and die;
"Twas ſo for me that Edwin did,
"And ſo for him will I."

"Forbid it, Heav'n!"(the Hermit cry'd,)
And claſp'd her to his Breaſt;
The wond'ring fair one turn'd to chide,
'Twas Edwin's ſelf that preſt.

"Turn, Angelina, ever dear,
"My Charmer, turn to ſee
"Thy own, thy long-loſt Edwin here,
"Reſtor'd to Love and thee.

"Thus let me hold thee to my Heart,
"And ev'ry Care reſign;
"And ſhall we never, never part,
"My Life—my all that's mine.

"No, never, from this Hour to part,
"We'll live, and love ſo true;
"The Sigh that rends thy conſtant Heart,
"Shall break thy Edwin's too."

THE HERMIT.

Turn, gentle Hermit of the Dale, and guide my lonely Way, to where yon Taper chears the Vale, with hof-pi-table Ray, Ray, For here, forlorn and loft, I tread, with fainting Steps and flow; where Wilds, immenfu-ra-bly fpread, feem length'ning as I go, feem length'ning as I go, feem length'-ning as I go.

Andantino

N⁰ 2.

For bear, my Son, the Her-mit cries, to tempt the dang'rous Gloom, for yonder faithlefs Phantom flies to lure thee to thy Doom. For bear, my Son, the Hermit cries, to tempt the dang'rous Gloom, for yonder faithlefs Phantom flies to lure thee to thy Doom; for yonder faithlefs Phantom flies to lure thee to thy Doom ___ to lure thee to thy Doom ___ to lure thee to thy Doom.

Volti Subito

4

Here to the houseless Child of Want, my Door is o-pen still ___; and tho' my Portion is but scant, and tho' my Portion is but scant, I give it with good Will, 'I give it with good Will,Then turn, to Night,and free-ly share what e'er my Cell be-stows, my ru-shy Couch,and frugal Fare,my Blessing and Re-pose; then turn to Night, and free-ly share,what e'er my Cell be-stows, my rushy Couch and frugal Fare,my Blessing and re-pose ___ my rushy Couch and fru-gal Fare,my

Blefsing and Re _ pofe _ _ _ my Blefsing and Re _ _ pofe _ _ _ my Blefsing and Re _

_pofe. No

Flocks that range the Valley free to Slaughter I con _ demn; taught by that Pow'r that

pities me, I learn to pi _ ty them. but from the Mountain's graffy Side a

guiltlefs Feaft I bring, a Scrip withHerbs and Fruit fupply'd,and Wa _ ter from the

Spring, _ and Wa _ ter from the Spring, and Wa _ ter from the Spring. Then

Volti Subito

6

Pilgrim, turn; thy Cares forego; all earth born Cares are wrong; Man wants but lit tle

here below, nor wants that little long. then, Pilgrim, turn; thy Cares forego; all

earth born Cares are wrong; Man wants but lit tle here below, nor wants that lit tle

long. Man wants but lit tle here below, nor wants that lit tle long, nor

wants that lit tle long nor wants that lit tle long.

Nº 3. Duetto

N.º 4. **Glee for three Voices.** NB. this may be fung as a fingle Song,

Far in a Wil - der - nefs ob - fcure the lone - ly, lone - ly

Far in a Wil - der - nefs ob - fcure the lone - ly, lone - ly

Far in a Wil - der - nefs ob - fcure the lone - ly, lone - ly

Vivace

Man - fion lay; a Refuge to the neighb'ring Poor, or Strangers led a - ftray; or

Man - fion lay; a Refuge to the neighb'ring Poor, or Strangers led a - ftray; or

Man - fion lay; a Refuge to the neighb'ring Poor, or Strangers led a - ftray; or

Stran - gers led a - ftray: a Refuge to the neighb'ring Poor, or Strangers led a -

Stran - gers led a - ftray: a Refuge to the neighb'ring Poor, or Strangers led a -

Stran - gers led a - ftray: a Refuge to the neighb'ring Poor, or Strangers led a -

- ftray. No Stores be - neath its hum - ble Thatch, no Stores beneath its

- ftray. No Stores be - neath its hum - - ble Thatch, no Stores be

- ftray. No Stores be - neath its hum - ble Thatch, no Stores beneath its

- ftray. No Stores be - neath its hum - ble Thatch, no Stores beneath its

Andantino Grazioso

Nº 5.

And now, when buſy Crowds retire, to take their Ev'ning Reſt, the Hermit trimm'd his little Fire, and chear'd his penſive Gueſt; and ſpread his ve - ge - table Store, and ſpread his ve-ge- table Store, and gayly preſt and ſmil'd; and, ſkill'd in ſegen - dary Lore, the ling'ring Hours be- guild - - the ling'ring Hours be - guild - - the ling'ring Hours beguil'd.

2

Around, in ſympathetic Mirth,
Its Tricks the Kitten tries;
The Cricket chirrups in the Hearth,
The crackling Faggot flies.
But Nothing could a Charm impart,
To ſooth the Stranger's Woe;
For Grief was heavy at his Heart,
And Tears began to flow.

Andantino

rifing Cares the Hermit fpy'd, with anfwring Care op-preft: and whence, un-happy Youth, he cry'd, the

Sorrows of thy Breaft? From better Ha-bi-tations fpurn'd, re-luctant doft thou rove; or

grieve for Friendfhip unreturn'd, or unre-guarded Love, - - or un-re guarded Love? A-

-las! the Joys that Fortune brings are trifling, and de-cay, and thofe, who prize the paltry Things, more

trifling far than they.

N.º 7.

Largo e Sempre Pianissimo

And what is Friendship, but a Name; a Charm that lulls to sleep; a Shade that fol-lows Wealth,or Fame, and leaves the Wretch to weep? and Love is still an emptier Sound, the modern fair one's Jest; on Earth un-seen, or only found to warm, to warm the Turtle's Nest: and what is Friendship, but a Name, a Charm that lulls to sleep, a Shade that fol-lows Wealth,or Fame, and leaves the Wretch to weep.

Recitative

For Shame, fond Youth, thy Sorrows hufh, and fpurn the Sex, he faid; but while he fpoke, a rifing blufh his lovelorn Gueft betray'd; a rifing Blufh his lovelorn Gueft betray'd.

N°. 8.

Vivace

Surpriz'd, he fees new Beauties rife, fwift mantling to the View, like Colours o'er the morning Skies, as bright, as tranfient too. The bafhful look, the rifing Breaft, alternate fpread Alarms; the lovely Stranger ftands confeft a Maid in all her Charms . . . a Maid in all her Charms, Charms.

14

N.º 9.

Largo

And ah! forgive a Stranger rude, a Wreth forlorn, she cry'd; whose Feet unhallow'd thus intrude where Heav'n and you re-fide. But let a Maid your Pity share, whom Love has taught to stray, who seeks for Rest, but finds Despair Com-panion of her Way; then, ah! forgive a Stranger rude, a Wretch forlorn, she cry'd; whose Feet unhallow'd thus intrude where Heav'n and you re-fide ___ where Heav'n and you re-fide.

Andante

Nº 10.

My Father liv'd he_ _fide the Tyne, a wealthy Lord was he; and all his Wealth was mark'd as mine, he had but on_ _ly me; he had but on_ _ly me.

2
Tı win me from his tender Arms,
Encumber'd Suitors came;
Who pr ı̍d me for imputed Charms,
And felt, or feign'd a Flame.

3
Each Fair a mercenary Crowd
With richeſt Proffers ſtrove;
Among the reſt young Edwin bow'd,
But never talk'd of Love.

4
In humble ſimpleſt Habit clad,
No Wealth or Pow'r had he;
Wiſdom and Worth were all he had;—
But theſe were all to me.

5
The Bloſſom op'ning to the Day,
The Dews of Heav'n refin'd,
Could nought of Purity diſplay,
To emulate his Mind.

6
The Dew, the Bloſſoms of the Tree,
With Charms inconſtant ſhine;
Their Charms were his, but woe to me,
Their Conſtancy was mine.

7
For ſtill I try'd each fickle Art,
Importunate and vain;
And while his Paſsion touch'd my Heart,
I triumph'd in his Pain.

8
'Till quite dejected with my Scorn,
He left me to my Pride,
And ſought a Solitude forlorn,
In ſecret, where he dy'd.

9
But mine the Sorrow, mine the Fault,
And well my Life ſhall pay;
I'll ſeek the Solitude he ſought,
And ſtretch me where he lay.

10
And there forlorn, deſpairing hid,
I'll lay me down and die;
'Twas ſo for me that Edwin did,
And ſo for him will I.

own, thy own, thy long-lost Edwin here, re_ftor'd to Love and thee ___ re_

_ftor'd to Love and thee ___ re_ftor'd to Love and thee. Thus let me hold thee

to my Heart, thus let me hold thee to my Heart, and ev _ 'ry Care, ev'ry Care re _ fign,

and fhall we ne_ver. never part, my Life, my Life, my all that's mine ___

___ my Life, my Life, my

all, my all that's mine, my Life, my Life, my all that's mine.

Angelina

Volti Subito

Angelina

We never from this Hour will part, We never from this Hour will part, we'll

Edwin

We never from this Hour will part, We never from this

live, well live, and love so true; the Sigh that rends thy con‒stant Heart, the

Hour will part,well live, and love so true; the

Sigh that rends thy con‒stant Heart, shall break,shall break Ange‒li‒na's too; ‒ ‒ ‒

Sigh that rends thy con‒stant Heart, shall break,shall break thy Ed‒win's too;

FINIS.